Look at Me!

Robert Munsch
Look at Me!

Illustrated by
Michael Martchenko

SCHOLASTIC CANADA LTD.
New York Toronto London Auckland Sydney
Mexico City New Delhi Hong Kong Buenos Aires

The illustrations in this book were painted in watercolour on Crescent illustration board.
The type is set in 24 point Ehrhardt MT Rg.

Scholastic Canada Ltd.
604 King Street West, Toronto, Ontario M5V 1E1, Canada

Scholastic Inc.
557 Broadway, New York, NY 10012, USA

Scholastic Australia Pty Limited
PO Box 579, Gosford, NSW 2250, Australia

Scholastic New Zealand Limited
Private Bag 94407, Greenmount, Auckland, New Zealand

Scholastic Children's Books
Euston House, 24 Eversholt Street, London NW1 1DB, UK

Library and Archives Canada Cataloguing in Publication
Munsch, Robert N., 1945-

Look at me! / Robert Munsch ; illustrated by Michael Martchenko.
ISBN 978-0-545-99431-6

I. Martchenko, Michael   II. Title.
PS8576.U575L58 2008a   jC813'.54   C2007-905724-1

ISBN-10 0-545-99431-4

8 7 6 5 4   Printed in Canada   09 10 11 12 13

FSC

Mixed Sources
Product group from well-managed
forests and other controlled sources
www.fsc.org Cert no. SGS-COC-003098
© 1996 Forest Stewardship Council

For Madison Snow,
Orangeville, Ontario
— R.M.

When Madison's grandma came to visit, everyone decided to go for a walk downtown.

In front of city hall, Madison said, "Look! Look! Look! I found a ticket – a ticket for free face painting at the park."

"Neat," said Madison's grandma. "Let's go to the park."

At the park, Madison got in a long, long line.

A girl came and said, "Get a scary face like mine."

"No," said Madison.

A boy came and said, "Get a tiger face like mine."

"No," said Madison.
A girl came and said, "Get a
butterfly face like mine."
"NO," said Madison.

Finally it was Madison's turn.

"I want," said Madison, "just on my cheek, a small, perfect rose that looks really real."

"Really real?" said the face painter.

"Really real!" said Madison, and the face painter spent a long, long time painting a small, perfect rose that looked really real.

"That's a nice flower," said Madison's dad. "Now let's go look in some stores."

At the hardware store, when her father was looking at drills and saws, Madison whispered, "Daddy! I think my flower is growing."

"That's nice," said her father.

"Daddy," whispered Madison. "Look! Look! Look! Please really LOOK at me. My flower is growing! There was just one rose, and now there are two."

Madison's father looked very closely at Madison's face and said, "Why, there really *are* two roses, one on each cheek! But I think it was that way already."

At the kitchen store, when her mother was looking at pots and pans, Madison said, "Mommy! My flower is growing."

"That's nice," said Madison's mother.

"Mommy," said Madison. "Look! Look! Look! Please really LOOK at me! My flower is growing! There was just one rose, and now there are three."

Madison's mother looked very closely at Madison's face and said, "Why, there *are* three roses! I thought you just asked for one."

"I did ask for one rose," said Madison.

"Well, I guess that face painter gave you three," said Madison's mother.

At the ice cream shop, Madison said, "Grandma! My flower is growing."

"That's nice," said Madison's grandma.

"Grandma!" said Madison. "Look! Look! Look! Please really LOOK at me! My flower is growing! There was one rose, and now there are twenty-four . . . and I think a leaf is growing out my ear!"

Then Madison turned over her arms. Ten roses were going down each arm, and while her grandma looked, another rose grew on the end of each stem.

"One rose was nice," said Madison. "Twenty-six is too many."

"This is serious!" said Madison's grandma, and she picked up Madison and ran down the street to the doctor's office.

The doctor was no help. She said, "I know a lot about people, but not a lot about plants."

"Let's try the garden store," said Madison.

At the garden store, the man behind the counter said, "Weed poison! Check out our Wonderful Weed Whomper!"

"AAAAAAAAAAAAHHHHHHHHH!"
yelled Madison. "No Weed Whomper."

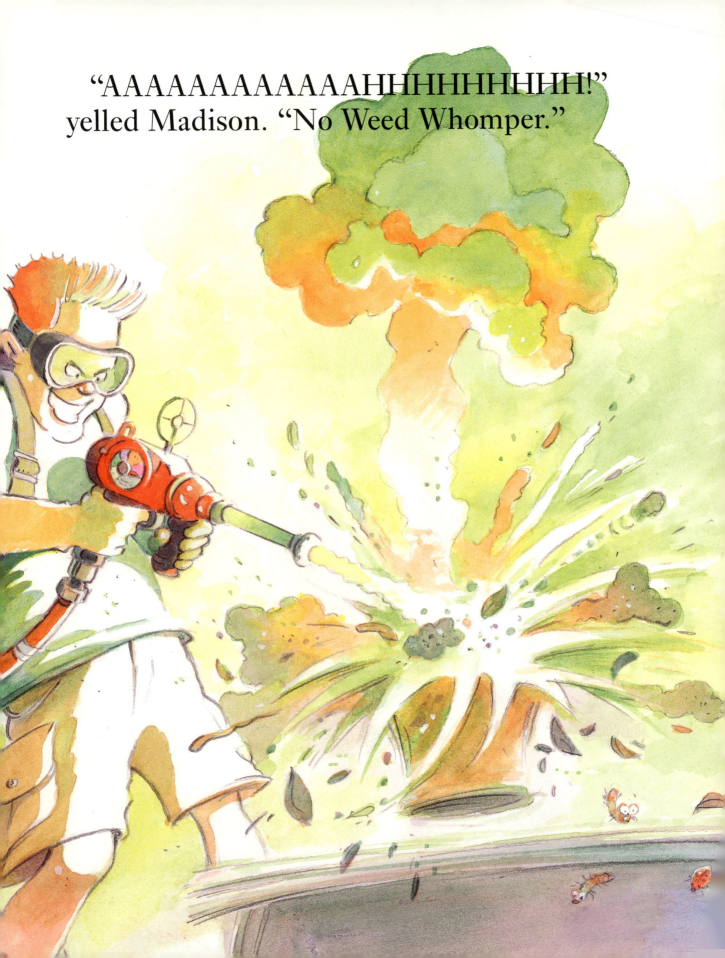

"I know," said Madison. "Let's be nice to the rose. I will go home and take a nap with a large flower pot beside my bed, and maybe the rose will go and live in the flower pot."

When Madison
woke up, there was
a huge rose bush
in the flower pot,
and just one
perfect rose
on her cheek.

Madison's
grandma took the
rose bush home
and planted it in
her garden, where
it stayed until it
found a better
place to grow.